Dear Parents:

Congratulations! Your child is taking the first steps on an exciting journey. The destination? Independent reading!

STEP INTO READING® will help your child get there. The program offers five steps to reading success. Each step includes fun stories and colorful art or photographs. In addition to original fiction and books with favorite characters, there are Step into Reading Non-Fiction Readers, Phonics Readers and Boxed Sets, Sticker Readers, and Comic Readers—a complete literacy program with something to interest every child.

Learning to Read, Step by Step!

Ready to Read   Preschool–Kindergarten
• big type and easy words • rhyme and rhythm • picture clues
For children who know the alphabet and are eager to begin reading.

Reading with Help   Preschool–Grade 1
• basic vocabulary • short sentences • simple stories
For children who recognize familiar words and sound out new words with help.

Reading on Your Own   Grades 1–3
• engaging characters • easy-to-follow plots • popular topics
For children who are ready to read on their own.

Reading Paragraphs   Grades 2–3
• challenging vocabulary • short paragraphs • exciting stories
For newly independent readers who read simple sentences with confidence.

Ready for Chapters   Grades 2–4
• chapters • longer paragraphs • full-color art
For children who want to take the plunge into chapter books but still like colorful pictures.

STEP INTO READING® is designed to give every child a successful reading experience. The grade levels are only guides; children will progress through the steps at their own speed, developing confidence in their reading.

Remember, a lifetime love of reading starts with a single step!

Special thanks to Ryan Ferguson, Debra Mostow Zakarin, Kristine Lombardi, Rita Lichtwardt, Nicole Corse, Karen Painter, Stuart Smith, Sammie Suchland, Charnita Belcher, Julia Phelps, Julia Pistor, Renata Marchand, Michelle Cogan, and Kris Fogel

Published in the United States by Random House Children's Books, a division of Penguin Random House LLC, 1745 Broadway, New York, NY 10019, and in Canada by Penguin Random House Canada Limited, Toronto.

Step into Reading, Random House, and the Random House colophon are registered trademarks of Penguin Random House LLC.

Visit us on the Web!
StepIntoReading.com
randomhousekids.com

Educators and librarians, for a variety of teaching tools, visit us at RHTeachersLibrarians.com

ISBN 978-1-101-93995-6 (trade) — ISBN 978-1-101-93996-3 (lib. bdg.) — ISBN 978-1-101-93997-0 (ebook)

Printed in the United States of America
10 9 8 7 6 5 4 3 2

Horses to the Rescue

Adapted by Devin Ann Wooster

Based on the screenplay by

Amy Wolfram and Kacey Arnold

Illustrated by Patrick Ian Moss

and The Artful Doodlers

Random House New York

Chelsea flies to an island
for a dance contest.

Her sisters and their
puppies go, too.

There is a horse show
on the island.
Marco the trainer
rides Spirit.

Vivian trains Beauty.

Beauty dances.

The puppies dance, too!

They chase butterflies.

The puppies find an SUV.

It pulls the horse trailer.

The trainers drive away.

The puppies go, too!

The sisters must
find the lost puppies.
They follow the SUV.

Their cart gets stuck.

They have

to camp out.

The sisters camp
under the stars.
Barbie points
to the North Star.

The other stars move.

The North Star
always points north.

The next morning,
the girls hike
to find the puppies.
They zip down a cliff.

Chelsea is worried.

She wants to get

to the dance contest.

The girls

find the puppies!

The puppies

kiss the girls.

Chelsea is late
for her dance contest!
Vivian and Marco
will drive everyone.

Uh-oh!

The bridge is out.

The horses want
to help!
They can take the girls
to the dance contest.

The girls ride
the horses.
They are lost.
They cannot find
the dance stage.

The girls

see the North Star.

The dance stage is north.

They follow the star!

The girls reach
the dance contest.
Chelsea dances.
Her sisters dance, too.

The horses dance.

The puppies dance.

Everyone dances!

Thanks to her sisters
and her friends,
Chelsea wins the contest!